book belongs to

. . . .

For Mum and Dad, and for Neil ~ E.S.

First published in Great Britain 2010
by Egmont UK Limited
239 Kensington High Street, London W8 6SA

Text and illustrations copyright © Ellie Sandall
The moral rights of the author/illustrator have been asserted

ISBN 978 1 4052 4737 5 (Hardback)
ISBN 978 1 4052 4738 2 (Paperback)

1 3 5 7 9 10 8 6 4 2

A CIP catalogue record for this title is available from the British Library

Printed and bound in Singapore

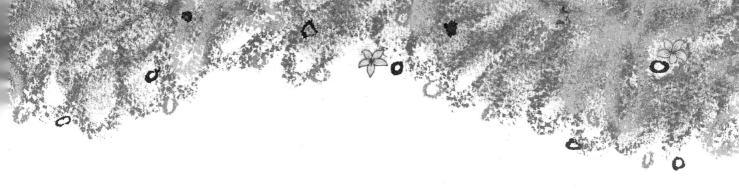

BIRDSONG

Ellie Sandall

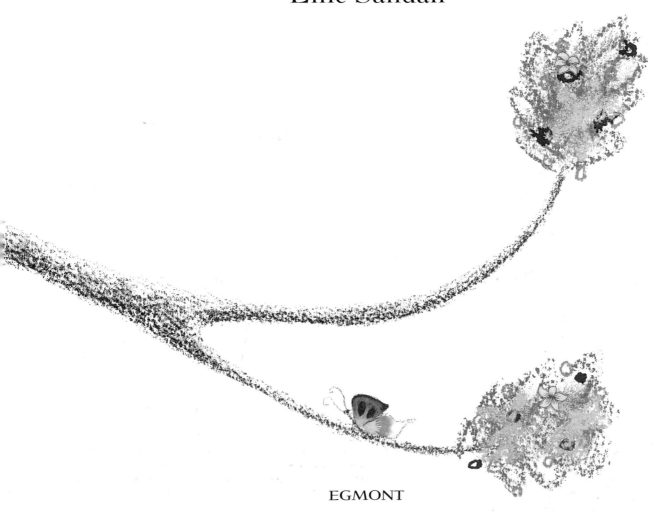

EGMONT

One small bird, in a tree.

Kitcha
kitcha
Kee
kee
kee

Here's another.
Come and see!

Urrah!
Urrah!
Rah
rah
ree

Two more pairs of landing feet.
Two more friendly birds to greet.

Chucka chucka Weet weet weet

Tchikka tchikka Tweet tweet tweet

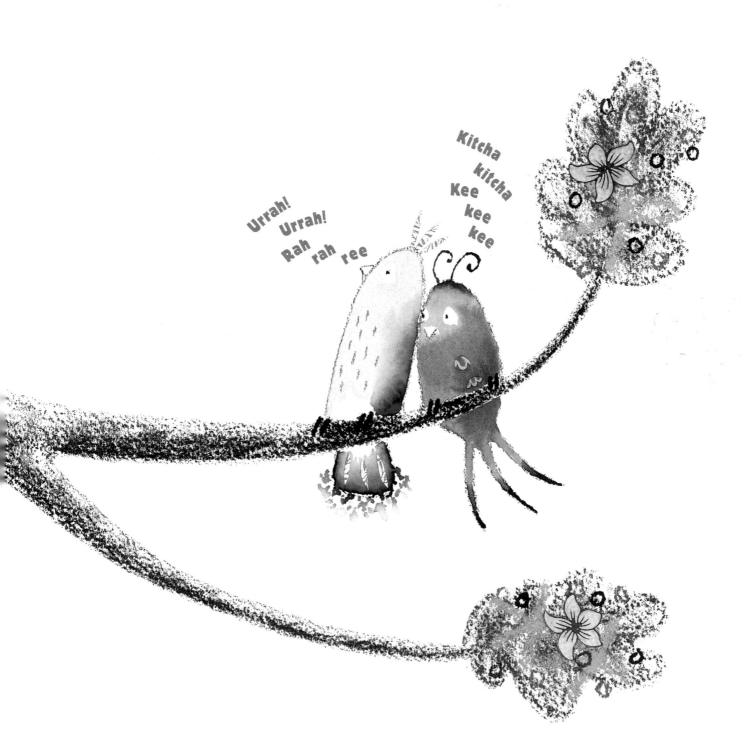

And now an owl's
come into view.

Too-whit
too-whit
too-whit
too-woo

Here's a parrot,
brown and blue.

Ru-tu
ru-tu
ru-tu-tu!

What a crowd!
What a crew!

Too-whit
too-whit
too-whit too-woo

Chucka
chucka
weet
weet
weet

Tchikka
tchikka
Tweet
tweet
tweet

Urrah! Urrah!
Rah rah ree

Kitcha kitcha
Kee kee
kee

What a truly splendid view,
and what a noise they're making too!

Two more birds
have made the trip.

Kirri!
Kirri!

Kip
kip
kip

Ru-tu ru-tu ru-tu-tu!

Too-whit too-whit too-whit too-woo

Chucka chucka

Weet weet weet

Tchikka tchikka
Tweet tweet tweet

Urrah! Urrah! Rah rah ree

Kitcha kitcha
Kee kee kee

Can any more fit on this tree?
It looks a little full to me!

All is quiet. All is still.
Not a sound.

At least until . . .

A huge bird with a mighty beak
joins them with
    a piercing shriek!

Now this bird thinks his job is done.
The little branch is all his own.

He hasn't seen
        the butterfly,
gently, gently
        floating by . . .

Look out, bird!

She softly lands
and in a flash –

CRaCK

CRaSH!

Oh.

The biggest bird,
the loudest call . . .

. . . but whatever could
have made him fall?